Goat and Donkey
in The Great Outdoors

For Gordon Littlejohn – S.P.
For Mark and Sean, 'brothers and friends' – R.J.

OXFORD
UNIVERSITY PRESS

Great Clarendon Street, Oxford OX2 6DP

Oxford University Press is a department of the University of Oxford.
It furthers the University's objective of excellence in research, scholarship,
and education by publishing worldwide in

Oxford New York
Auckland Cape Town Dar es Salaam Hong Kong Karachi
Kuala Lumpur Madrid Melbourne Mexico City Nairobi
New Delhi Shanghai Taipei Toronto

With offices in
Argentina Austria Brazil Chile Czech Republic France Greece
Guatemala Hungary Italy Japan Poland Portugal Singapore
South Korea Switzerland Thailand Turkey Ukraine Vietnam

Oxford is a registered trade mark of Oxford University Press
in the UK and in certain other countries

Text copyright © Simon Puttock 2007
Illustrations copyright © Russell Julian 2007

The moral rights of the author and artist have been asserted

Database right Oxford University Press (maker)

First published 2007

Reissued in 2008

British Library Cataloguing in Publication Data available

ISBN: 978-0-19-272844-9 (Paperback)

10 9 8 7 6 5 4 3 2 1

Printed in China

Paper used in the production of this book is a natural, recyclable
product made from wood grown in sustainable forests. The manufacturing
process conforms to the environmental regulations of the country of origin.

Simon Puttock and Russell Julian

Goat and Donkey
in The Great Outdoors

OXFORD
UNIVERSITY PRESS

One morning Goat announced, 'I have decided to go on a holiday. A camping holiday in the Great Outdoors!' 'What a good idea,' said Donkey. 'And while you are away I will have lots of peace and quiet to read my book.'

'Goody,' said Goat, 'so that's all settled then.'
But –

'Donkey,' said Goat a little while later, 'where do you think I should GO on my camping holiday?'
'Goodness,' said Donkey. 'Haven't you decided yet?'
'Not REALLY,' said Goat. 'I want to go somewhere very special, but I don't know where. Will you help me?'

'Well,' said Donkey, 'perhaps you should decide what SORT of place you'd like to go to, first. For instance, would you like a hot place, or a cold place?'

Goat did not want to be TOO hot, and he did not want to be TOO cold. 'Somewhere in between,' he said.

'And do you want to get wet, or do you want to stay dry?' asked Donkey.

Goat liked being wet sometimes,
and sometimes he liked being dry.
'A bit of both, please,' he said.

'And how about somewhere high up,
or somewhere low down?' asked Donkey.
High up made Goat feel giddy and
low down could be scary and
underground. 'Flat in the middle
would be grand,' he decided.

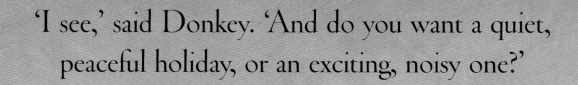

'I see,' said Donkey. 'And do you want a quiet,
peaceful holiday, or an exciting, noisy one?'

'Goodness,' said Goat. 'I give up! There's lots
more to the Great Outdoors than I realised!
I will think about it and let you know.'

At lunch Goat said, 'Donkey, I have thought and thought, and I have decided that I would like to go somewhere just like here. Do you know a special place that is just like here?'

Donkey thought hard. 'Goat,' he said at last,
'there is only one special place in the world that is
Just Like Here.'

'Goody,' said Goat,
'then that is where I will go.'
And he trotted off to
finish his packing.

'But Goat,' said Donkey, 'that special place IS here!'
'Goody and goody and gumdrops,' said Goat.
'Then I will have my camping holiday in
the Great Outdoors RIGHT HERE!
I will put up my tent in the garden
and everything will be perfect.'

Donkey spent all afternoon helping
Goat to put up his tent in the
middle of the garden.

Then Goat snuggled down in his sleeping bag
and listened to the quiet.
Perhaps, he thought, it is a little TOO quiet.
I do not like things being too noisy,
but I do not like them being
too quiet, either.

'Donkey!' Goat called.
'Yes, Goat?' said Donkey.
'I'm thinking . . .' said Goat.
'What are you thinking?'

'I am thinking that I'm feeling a bit TOO QUIET on my own,' said Goat. 'Perhaps you'd like to join me in the Great Outdoors?'

'Well,' said Donkey, 'can I bring my book with me?
And some games? And my very special blanket?'
'That sounds like a Very Good Idea,' said Goat.
'In that case,' said Donkey, 'I'd love to join you.'
Donkey squashed into the tent and snuggled down, too.

'Donkey,' said Goat.
'Yes, Goat?' said Donkey.

'I think perhaps it is still too quiet. What shall we do?'
'I know,' said Donkey, 'we could play catch.'

But it is very difficult to play catch in a tent.

And almost impossible to play football.
And trying to play ping pong in a tent is just plain SILLY!

'Phew!' said Goat. 'I am all tired out!
Perhaps we ought to do something QUITE quiet, after all.'
'I know what,' said Donkey, 'would you like me to tell you a story?'
'I like stories!' said Goat.
'Shall we snuggle down and have an exciting adventure story?
A story about the Great Outdoors?'
'Oh, goody,' said Goat, 'yes, let's!'

So that is exactly what they did.